WORD

WORD

A Real Dog Locked in a Shelter
Cage for Eight Years Until...

Florence Petheram

A Division of WINEPRESS PUBLISHING

Pleasant Word (a division of WinePress Publishing, PO Box 428, Enumclaw, WA 98022) functions only as book publisher. As such, the ultimate design, content, editorial accuracy, and views expressed or implied in this work are those of the author.

ISBN 1-4141-0518-5
Library of Congress Catalog Card Number: 2005905608

Dedication

F or children of all ages who dearly love their dogs and other animals—and especially for my children, Paula, Robin, Julie, and Scott.

A Few Words
about Word

This is a story about a dog named Word, based on an article from *The Seattle Times*.

Word was a real dog. Judy Woods and Sierra Ravenwolf are real people. Cochise Sunbear is a real wolf. The Pigs Peace Sanctuary is a real place located in Stanwood, Washington, where Judy takes loving care of many other animals besides her pigs. The Website is www.pigspeace.org

Along the way of writing about Word, I owe special thanks to the following people for their contributions to the story: Harlan Dorfman, attorney, who knew firsthand about the trials of the real Word; Virginia Dallon, animal care supervisor, Seattle Animal Shelter; Sergeant Chris Meyer, Animal Control, King County; Adam Karp, animal rights lawyer; Nancy Muldoon, for her writing advice; author Esther Mae Hamel, for inspiration; Bette Lepp, for proofing and encouragement; Alaska Airlines Pilot John Severski, for making my computer fly right; Peggy King Anderson, for professional writing advice; and Rusty, our Golden Retriever, who hung around my desk with good doggy support while the story was written.

Because of my love for Word, I've changed names and added fictional events. Word didn't mind at all.

Table of Contents

Chapter 1: First There Was Word 11

Chapter 2: New Fears 15

Chapter 3: An Unhappy Change 21

Chapter 4: Help Arrives 27

Chapter 5: Time Runs Out 31

Chapter 6: Just in Time 35

Chapter 7: A New Life 39

Chapter 8: A Different World 43

Chapter 9: Heart Break 47

Chapter 10: Sierra Returns 51

Chapter 11: A Friend in Trouble 55

Chapter 12: Disaster 59

Chapter 13: The Unexpected 65

CHAPTER 1

First There Was Word

A little nudge was all it took, and a gate that should have been locked swung open. Slowly at first, then two black streaks raced through.

The black streaks were the dogs Word and his mama, Parsheba. Like two naughty kids they scampered down the sidewalk into the bright spring morning on their way to fun and freedom! Down the sidewalk they marched. Word, with his feather-like tail waving like a flag, pranced happily alongside his mama. They weren't supposed to be out of the yard, but it was such a great feeling to be out from behind the locked gate.

They had only gone a couple of blocks when suddenly, WHAM! Without warning, two large ladies burst forth onto the sidewalk, crashing into Word and Parsheba. Both ladies lost their balance and screamed as they crumpled onto the stunned dogs. A wild jumble of legs, arms, black fur, and polka dots mingled with screams and animal cries.

The largest lady, wearing a polka dot dress, landed on top of Word.

"Ooooooo," groaned the lady, as she cried out, "Oh no, no, no!"

"Yoww!" barked Word as he painfully crawled from the pile. Parsheba managed to struggle to her front legs. When she saw what had happened to Word she did what any animal mother would do to protect her young, she fought back. No one was going to hurt her Word! With a furious snarl and growl, she lunged and tried to nip at the ankles of the lady who had fallen closest. That caused more screams of terror.

"Help! Get away from me, get away! Let go of me! Oh, someone please help!" The lady kicked wildly at Parsheba from where she had fallen. The more she kicked, the more Parsheba snapped and lunged, scaring the lady even more. The women's cries caused neighbors to come running from every direction.

One man cried out, "Keep away from those dogs! They're vicious and dangerous! Quick! Someone call 911."

Another man yelled, "Where's a stick or board? I'll fix those dogs. It's getting so we're not safe in our own neighborhood anymore."

Word pulled free from the tangle and, panting heavily, crawled back on the grass. Very frightened and with heart pounding, he wobbled back down the sidewalk, trying to get away as fast as possible. Parsheba, limping badly, followed him. Word looked back. He could see the lady in the polka dot dress being helped to her feet by neighbors. The other lady was still on the ground crying. By now more people had gathered around. Some were pointing their fingers at the dogs and shaking their heads.

Word knew something really bad was sure to come from all of this. He could feel it, and he could smell it. There was a different scent in the air when things weren't right. For sure, they weren't right now. He was worried about Mama's limping. She was hurt from the lady kicking her so hard. He could tell she was in pain, and he didn't feel so good himself. This was the worst thing that had ever happened to him.

Oh, how he wished he and Mama had never left home. They both knew they shouldn't leave the yard. If only the gate had been locked like it was supposed to be, this terrible thing would never have happened. Whip, the man they lived with, always told them to stay in the yard. They should have listened. But it was too late now. Word wished he and Mama were on Whip's warm lap in front of the TV. Instead, a cold fear crept through him. He sensed a change in his life he had never felt before. It was a sick feeling, and right then he didn't know what to do or where to go. What should they do? There was only one thing to do for now, and that was to keep right on going.

And so they did.

CHAPTER 2

New Fears

W ord did not see the white truck with the words TRI-COUNTY ANIMAL SHELTER cruising down the street a few blocks behind them. He did not know the two uniformed men inside, Chris and Pete, field officers from the shelter, had been alerted about the accident. They had both worked for the shelter for years and had been hired, not only because they liked animals, but also because they had a way with animals and people. They were kind men. They knew their job was not just to pick up dogs and cats, but to be "problem solvers" as well. As long as there were people and animals, they knew there would always be problems. And this day, that's what they were about to do--solve a problem. The problem was Word and Parsheba.

Word and Parsheba had slowed down quite a bit by now. Parsheba was whining as she limped down the sidewalk, her tail dragging. Word was keeping pace a little ahead of her. He was hurting too, but he wanted to get as far away as possible from that horrible accident.

"There they are," said Officer Chris. "Those dogs sure look alike. They must be from the same litter."

"Yeah," said Officer Pete, "it sounds like they were double trouble today for someone. One of them looks hurt."

The men jumped out of the truck, and Officer Pete grabbed a come-a-long pole. The come-a-long pole was made of aluminum and looked like a fishing pole with a loop at the end. The loop went over the head of the animal and could then be tightened by a cord on the pole. In this way, the animal could be captured while the officer stayed at a safe distance in case the animal attacked.

"This should be easy," said Officer Pete. And for Parsheba it was. Word, while still scampering, saw Parsheba "looped" with only a whimper as the loop settled over her head. He slowed down a little as he watched Officer Pete safely secure Parsheba in one of the compartments in the back of the truck. Word felt great alarm as the attention shifted to him.

"Be careful!" called Officer Chris. "Remember, the complaint said these dogs are vicious biters and very dangerous."

Word was not to be caught so easily. He ran off down the sidewalk, veered into a yard, and surprised the officers by turning and running in the opposite direction. He began heading straight for home where he knew he would be safe. This time his path took him through back yards instead of the sidewalk. Panting heavily from running, he finally arrived at the gate to his yard, safe for now, he thought.

Word felt great relief the minute he saw Whip. Whip was standing on the sidewalk with his hands on his hips looking anxiously up and down the street. This was the man who loved and cared for him and Mama, and a man the neighbors called "a good guy."

Whip was tall and thin with a mop of white hair and deep, dark-blue eyes. He had served in the U.S. Marine Corps years ago and got around pretty well except for a limp caused from being wounded in the war.

Word felt safe now that he had reached home. He knew Whip would take care of this bad problem and make it go away. Whip reached down to scratch Word's head and said in a cross but loving way, "Where did you two go? I've been looking all over for you. You know you're not supposed to leave this yard. Now where's Parsheba?"

Word knew where Parsheba was. She was in a truck on the street. And that truck was now moving slowly and quietly like a giant bug until it stopped in front of Whip.

It had not been hard to follow the fleeing Word. The officers had a pretty good idea from their years of experience that Word would probably head for home.

Anxiously, Word watched as both officers got out of the truck and calmly approached Whip. "Is this your dog, sir?" asked Officer Chris, pointing at Word.

"Yeah, it is. Why?" demanded Whip. "And where is Parsheba, my other dog?"

"We have the other one," Officer Chris said, nodding his head toward the truck.

Word was still anxious as the men questioned Whip and heard Whip's answers become louder and angrier.

"I must inform you, sir, that your two dogs have been accused of attacking and biting two ladies who required medical care," Officer Chris reported. "We have a signed complaint. Also, there were several witnesses. We have to take the dogs in now. Here is a copy of the County and State dog laws and a copy of your rights," he said, as he handed Whip a bunch of papers. "This is serious business, sir. Do you understand that? Also, I'm sorry to say, our computer shows this is not the first time. There have been other complaints against your dogs."

"I don't care what your old computers say. My dogs do not bite, and they are not vicious. If somebody says they are, they're lying!" yelled Whip. When Whip started yelling, Word knew things were bad and moved closer to him. He watched Whip looking grim and silent as the officers explained to him his rights and where the dogs would be taken.

Suddenly, in a move that surprised everyone, Officer Pete "looped" Word and dragged him to the back of the truck. Word, completely caught off guard by the sudden capture, did not have time to make a sound or see an angry Whip limp down the sidewalk after him.

One minute Word was on the sidewalk and the next he was locked in the safety pen in the truck. In shock, Word and Parsheba watched Whip raise his fist in the air and yell something. Then, the truck door slammed shut!

"You know," said Pete as they drove off, "I get the feeling that's a nice guy back there who really loves those dogs but just doesn't quite get it."

"Yeah," said Chris, "I think you're right. Remember what we always say, *it's never the dog's fault.*"

From the window in the truck, a terrified Word and Parsheba barked and howled as they watched their beloved Whip fade from view.

Word could not know that because of an unlocked gate, his life would never be the same again.

CHAPTER 3

An Unhappy Change

lthough his heart was still pounding loudly, Word
lay quietly with his head on his paws, his tail flat
behind him. One unusual thing about Word was
his black eyes. If you looked closely, you got a funny feeling Word knew everything that was going on around him
and could understand what people were saying. Those
black eyes were now taking in the whole area where he and
Mama had been placed. They were in the special section of
the animal shelter behind the chain where dangerous dogs
and other dogs with legal problems were kept. In this area
no one except special shelter workers was allowed. The
only comfort to Word was that Mama was in a locked cage
beside him. Whining softly, she had fallen asleep soon after
being placed in the cage.

Still without moving, Word watched as two young men
entered the area. They wore the same pale green animal
shelter uniforms with matching caps that the officers, Chris

and Pete, wore. Both had a nice and kindly appearance. He didn't know what to expect from them, so he lay perfectly still. Now on his guard, his eyes watched their every move and heard every word. He waited for something to happen. Not a hair on his body moved.

"Rich, put food and water in those two cages over there. We have some new guests," said Vic, the tall one, pointing at Word. "But be careful, and I mean really careful! This one and Parsheba just came in and they're dangerous. I hear they bit a couple of ladies who ended up in the emergency room at the hospital."

Rich, wary of a possible attack from Word, unlocked the kennel door and slowly placed a clean bowl of food and fresh water inside. He studied Word for a long time. Then said quietly, "Hey, ole buddy, here's something to eat. Come on, eat this, you'll feel better. You don't look very dangerous to me. Maybe it's all a mistake. Maybe you can go home soon. You look like a nice fellow to me. Come on now and eat up."

Still, Word did not move. He was neither hungry nor thirsty. He was full of a numb fear. All he wanted was to go home with Mama and curl up on Whip's lap in front of the TV.

Within a day or two, Word became used to the routine at the shelter and calmed down. It helped that Parsheba was in the next cage so they could touch noses and feel close, but she mostly slept all day and night. Like all the animals at the shelter, Word and Parsheba were fed and their cages cleaned at the same time every day. Word had come to know and expect those times. But always, he and Parsheba were kept in their cages behind the chain. They were walked in the "shelter run," but never allowed outside! From his cage behind the chain, Word saw dogs brought in hurt, crying, and very scared. They did not know why they were there, and their howls were pitiful. But most of the dogs settled down to the regular schedule unless they were lucky enough to go home right away. Some dogs liked being there because it was the first time in their lives they had regular food, water, and shelter. Other dogs let out heartbreaking howls as they sat at the doors of their cages waiting for someone to come for them.

Word did not like being in a cage all the time. He waited for Whip to come and take him and Mama home so they could all be together again. That was not to be, but lucky for Word, someone was there to make life a lot easier.

Her name was Carol. She wore jeans, a white T-shirt, had short brown hair, and worked behind the chain. Word liked and trusted Carol at once. Her voice was warm and assuring and melted most of Word's fears. "Hello, young man," she said in a cheery voice, stooping down and placing her face close to his cage. "I'll bet you're wondering why you and Parsheba are here and when you can go home. Sorry, I can't answer everything, but Whip, your daddy, called to ask about you. I told him I'd keep a special eye out for you. He really loves you and Parsheba and said to tell you he's figuring out a way to get you back home. And I found out how you got your name too. He told me that when you were born a lady saw you and said, 'My word, what a beautiful puppy!' and that's how you became Word."

For the first time since being there, Word was encouraged by Carol's presence. He understood by her tone and mood that there was hope, and he showed it by prancing around the cage, tail wagging, ears at attention, with a doggy smile on his face.

As the days went by, Carol became more important to Word and Parsheba. She brought in a toy for each, and when no one was looking, sneaked special treats of liver chips just for Word. Each day he waited to hear her voice. She talked to him about all kinds of things as she brushed him and held him in her arms. She talked to Word as if he were human and told him things he did not know. "Word, did you know that you're a kind of a dog called a Lhasa Apso (la'sa ap'so)? Your long-ago ancestors were used as inside guard dogs in monasteries and palaces because they were so smart. You should feel very proud, Word, because you're smart too. I'll bet you're even smarter."

As the weeks went by she told him more about Whip and a man by the name of Tom who was fighting with the city over what was going to happen to him and Mama. "Oh, Word," she said softly as she stroked the little bit of white hair around his nose and chin.

"There's a big fight going on about you two. The city prosecutor says that you and Parsheba are vicious and should be put to death because you're a danger to society. And Whip and his attorney Tom say that it was all a big mistake. They say that because Whip served our country in the Marines, he should be allowed to keep his family, which is you and your mama."

Word loved and understood when she talked about Whip, but the rest of what she said left him feeling very nervous.

Early one morning when Carol came behind the chain, Word noticed she went directly to Parsheba's cage first. That was unusual because Mama was still asleep and hadn't greeted him yet with her usual sniffs and snorts. She just lay there with her legs out stiff. Her body lay perfectly still. This was not like Mama. What was happening?

Word began pacing back and forth in his cage facing the motionless Parsheba. The minute Carol opened Parsheba's cage door he smelled it-- it came to him instantly. He knew exactly what it was, and it made him sick inside. He knew his mama would never greet him again or share the treats that Carol brought. Never again would the two of them curl up together on Whip's lap. A great sadness filled his little body! He knew his mama was dead!

Word let out a mournful howl that was heard throughout the shelter.

CHAPTER 4

Help Arrives

He had to do something. So Word tried, without success, to tear through the wire cage with his paws to get to Parsheba as she lay lifeless in the cage beside him. This was his mama, his friend. Now she was gone! Everything and everyone was gone; his mama, Whip, his home. And with that Word slumped down on all fours with his nose as close as possible to Parsheba's cage. His howls had turned into a whimpering cry, and a heavy feeling of fear and loss came over him.

By now, Carol had called for help. Rich and Vic appeared at once with a small stretcher to take away the dead Parsheba. "Too bad," said Rich, "What a way to go. I understand this dog had cancer."

Carol, who was helping, replied, "Yes, dogs get some of the same kinds of diseases we humans get. This one came to us already hurting. There was nothing we could do to save her except give her pain pills. At least she didn't suffer at the end. Right now the one who is suffering is Word." And she turned her head toward his pathetic whimpers.

Quickly she unlocked his cage and pulled the sad-looking Word into her arms. She rocked Word in her arms as if he were a baby. "I'm so sorry, Word. I'm sorry your mama is gone, but she isn't hurting anymore, and it's going to be OK. You'll see."

Word refused all food for several days after the death of his mama. He lay facing her empty cage, barely moving. Carol told him in a soft voice that animals, like people, mourn the loss of someone they love. "It can hurt inside for a long time," she told him, "but after awhile the hurt goes away. And it will for you too, Word."

For now the hurt was still inside as he looked sadly at the cage where his mama had lived. He could not understand why she was gone, even though he knew she had been hurting before the lady kicked her.

A few days later, when Word had calmed down, Carol was brushing him and told him Whip had called and was very sad about Parsheba but couldn't get to the shelter because he had no car and didn't drive. "Whip said to tell you he loved you and missed you very much and is trying to get you back home," she said brightly. She also told him that someone new would be working with him—someone he would like.

He listened and heard the name several times—Sierra Ravenwolf. Carol, in her friendly way with Word, began telling him all about Sierra Ravenwolf. "You have to know, Word, that Sierra has been assigned to work with you because she's an animal doctor here at the shelter, and she works with animals who have special needs. All that means is, because of the things that have happened to you lately, like the accident and losing your mama and all, you need some special help right now. Sierra is just the one to give it to you, Word. She's cool. You're going to love her. And, get this. She has a real honest-to-goodness wolf living with her! The wolf's name is Cochise Sunbear. She named him after two brave Indian chiefs. A few years ago, she saved the wolf from owners who had tortured and starved him. Cochise Sunbear ended up saving her after she had been in a bad car accident. I hear the wolf never left her side until she got well. Anyway, get ready for a new friend. She'll be here tomorrow."

Word was curious when, the next day, a lady with a soft, low voice approached his cage and said, "Hello, Word. My name is Sierra Ravenwolf. I've come to help you feel better. And I think we're going to become very good friends."

Word wagged his tail and stared back at his new friend. For Word, Sierra Ravenwolf couldn't have come at a better time. He was going to need all the friendship and help she could give him.

CHAPTER 5

Time Runs Out

Sierra Ravenwolf's long black hair and clear blue eyes were as beautiful as her soft voice. With this soft voice she called Word by name and told him more of why she was there. Gently, she carried him to the table where she worked behind the chain at the shelter. In the beginning she had explained to him that she was going to massage him with a nice smelling healing oil called Lavender. She said it was used on animals and people to help them relax. Each time Sierra rubbed the Lavender oil into his shoulders, ears, and the web part of his feet, she always added comforting words. "Oh, Word, I know we're not seeing the best of you here at the shelter, but I want you to know I'm here to help you. I'm going to make you feel a lot better. Just wait and see. In a little while you'll feel really good. How does that sound?"

Her fingers touched and smoothed out the sore places on his small frame. He listened as she talked about everything that had happened to him, repeating over and over how he was going to be OK. It was her talking he liked almost as much as the massage. He loved the sound of her voice and what she said to him. Her soft words always made him feel safe and calm.

Word paid close attention when she talked about her wolf, Cochise Sunbear, whom she had saved. He heard the anger in her voice as she told how the men who owned him kept him in a small, dirty cage and starved and beat him. "You know, Word," she said, "animals are a lot like people. They hurt, cry, worry, and even smile like people. It makes me furious when I hear stories about the cruelty of humans toward God's creatures. All animals are wonderful and beautiful in their special way. And just like us, they change when shown lots of love. That, my dear friend, is why I love treating animals, especially dogs like you. After animals have experienced something terribly upsetting, I get to see how their bodies and spirits change. You're a good example, Word. You've been here in the shelter a long time, and I've already seen some changes in you since we've been working together."

It was true. Sierra Ravenwolf had made a change in him. So far it was the best he had felt since living behind the chain at the shelter. His body felt better and so did his spirit. Just as he loved when Carol came around, he looked forward to Sierra Ravenwolf's visits. Sometimes when she was working on him she was quiet and didn't say anything. Word still understood her, because she was talking "heart talk." From her heart to his, she told him things without saying a word, and he understood back with his heart. That was the way between them. Because of Word's keen sense of smell, he always knew when Sierra Ravenwolf arrived at the shelter. The whiff of lavender announced her presence, and he always danced in his cage to greet her.

One day Sierra and Carol were talking in a disturbing way that caused Word to become upset. He didn't understand all of it, but he knew it had something to do with him.

"Sierra, did you hear the news?" asked Carol. "After all this time, the State Supreme Court has finally decided that Word is considered property and not human family. They say he's considered potentially dangerous, and that means..."

"I heard," said Sierra, with tears in her eyes. "I don't want Word to know any of this. Please don't say anything in front of him."

It was too late. A scary feeling had already come over Word. He could smell the difference in the air around him by the way Carol and Sierra Ravenwolf were talking. After all this time, a new old fear came creeping back.

He was right about the new fear. If he could have heard the rest of the conversation between Carol and Sierra, he would have learned that after several years, Whip and Tom, Whip's attorney, had finally lost the legal battle to save him. They had tried to prove the case that Whip considered Word to be family, not property, and therefore had special rights. The High Court had ruled otherwise and considered Word to still be a public danger. It further decreed that on a certain Friday at five o'clock, Word should be euthanized—put to death.

After eight long years at the shelter, time had finally run out for Word.

CHAPTER 6

Just in Time

Word's fears would have faded a little if he could have heard the conversation Tom, Whip's attorney, had with two people on a Monday morning.

The first call Tom made was to his friend Judy Woods, the manager of the Pigs' Peace Sanctuary, located about 75 miles out of town. He told her all about Word and asked if she would be willing to take Word if he could talk the prosecuting attorney into releasing Word to the sanctuary. Tom had chosen to ask Judy because she loved and cared for animals that had no other place to go. Her sanctuary began as a shelter for potbellied pigs but had grown to include many kinds of animals. He knew Word would be safe and happy there.

"I certainly will," she said. "No problem. We'll add him to the rest of our family of pigs, dogs, cats, horses, chickens, and two llamas. He'll fit right in. We have other dogs out here he can play with too. Let me know."

"Great," said Tom, "I knew I could count on you. Now if I can just convince someone else about Word, everything will be cool."

His next phone call was to the Tri-County Prosecutor. This is what Word would have heard Tom say: "About that legal problem we have with the dog, Word, what if we take him out of the county to an animal sanctuary and let him live the rest of his life out there? He won't be around people and besides, we all know we're not really positive it was Word who bit the lady anyway. It could have been the other dog, and we're not even sure the lady was really bitten." Tom added, "Come on. Let him go. We've spent too many years and too much money on this case. Honestly, it you could see this dog, you'd know there's not a vicious bone in his body. How about it? What do you say?"

After more discussion, the prosecutor agreed. And so it was, Word's life would be saved if Judy signed legal papers agreeing to take Word out of the Tri-County area and to never let him have contact with the general public. Furthermore, Word was to be fitted with an ID microchip. In case he ever got out of the sanctuary and was caught, he would be destroyed immediately. Legally, Word was still considered a dangerous animal. Also, part of the deal was that Judy had to be in the prosecutor's office by the end of the week on Friday to sign the papers before five o'clock. If not, a call to the shelter would end Word's life on Friday at five o'clock.

When the phone call came into the shelter office at exactly ten minutes to five on Friday afternoon, there was dead silence for a moment. Then the good news spread throughout the shelter like wildfire, as the whole place erupted like a volcano. Word was saved!

When Carol and Sierra Ravenwolf heard the news, they ran to Word's cage. It was in that split second when he saw them coming for him he knew his life had changed again. Word felt himself being gently lifted by Sierra. With tears and cheers she danced with him! This time it was on the other side of the chain. She sang out, "Word is free! Word is free! Word, you're going to a new home. You'll have other animal friends to play with. You won't have to be in a cage. You can run outside as much as you want. Word, you're free! You're free after eight long years!" With that, all the shelter workers started cheering and clapping! They set up such a loud commotion that the other shelter dogs caught the excitement and started barking and howling.

Word blinked his black eyes and felt new joyous energy all around him. Word felt in his heart that something very wonderful and special had just happened to him. He could smell it, hear it, and feel it. He wanted the feeling to last forever.

CHAPTER 7

A New Life

The sky was a dull, November gray as the van, with Sierra Ravenwolf, Carol, and Word, turned onto a country road headed for the sanctuary. As they passed farms tucked away in shadowy forests of pine and cedar, Word became more and more nervous. From his cage in the back of the van he could feel the old fears returning. This was the first time in many years he had been outside the animal shelter, and he couldn't figure out what was going on. Little did he know that his life had been saved by a miracle of minutes.

All along the way he heard Sierra Ravenwolf's comforting words. "Word, it's OK. We're going to your new home where you'll meet new friends. You can be outside as much as you want. Trust me, Word, you'll love it. I know you will."

If there was anyone Word could trust, it was Sierra Ravenwolf. She had cared for him at the shelter during the

past years in her special loving way. She understood what
he was thinking and knew he was not a vicious dog. With
her wolf-like blue eyes and warm touch, she had let Word
know that he was loved. But in spite of Sierra Ravenwolf's
reassuring words, the fear in him grew with each mile.

Finally they turned onto a muddy road and came to a
comfortable-looking two-story, white farmhouse. Tall pine
trees shaded the front porch. A wire fence safeguarded the
neat yard and surrounding acres. On the locked gate a sign
read: WELCOME TO THE PIGS PEACE SANCTUARY
WHERE ANIMALS LIVE IN PEACE AND LOVE.

The van stopped, and Carol got out first. As she was
unlocking the gate, she sang out, "We're here, Word! Here's
your new home, Word! We are here." During the years at
the shelter it was Carol who sneaked in special treats and
toys for Word. She had bathed, walked, and talked to him.
She told him about the happenings at the shelter and about
her life. Word loved how Carol talked to him. Like other
dogs, he understood words, tone of voice, and the meaning.
If people only knew how much dogs really understood they
might treat them differently. For this and all the rest, Word
had come to love Carol too.

"Wait at minute," Sierra Ravenwolf said to Carol. "I want
a few minutes alone with Word. Go ahead and introduce
yourself to Judy, and please take in Word's bed and toys."

With increasing concern, Word pranced nervously in
the cage. Eagerly he waited for Sierra to open the door of
the van. Carefully she picked him up and held him close
to her, gently stroking his head. She whispered in his ear,
"Word, this is your new home I was telling you about. This

will be so good for you, I promise. You're going to have a new happy adventure. You'll be free. Do you know what that means? You can be outside to run in the grass and feel the sun. Oh, Word, I'm glad for you but sad for me. Carol and I are going to miss you, sweet Word."

Holding him close to her cheek she stroked his soft body from head to tail and kissed his nose. In return, Word licked a tear from her face and wondered what was going to happen to him next.

Judy, seeing the van, came out of the farmhouse to greet them. She walked toward Sierra Ravenwolf who held Word. "Hello, Word," she said with a big smile. "Welcome to your new home. You're going to have fun here. There are other dogs to play with. There's Moses and Brian and Jake and Peter. You'll get to meet all the pigs, and there are a lot of them. See Tom, the turkey over by the fence? See the cats up in the loft?" She pointed in the direction of the barn. "Don't worry, they'll stay out of your way. You'll get to know the two llamas, Gus and Packer. And there are acres to run around in."

The tone of Judy's voice and new words meant, above all else, that he was going to be deserted by the people he loved—again. He struggled and whined as Sierra Ravenwolf gently tried to place him on the grass. Why was she trying to leave him in this strange place with strange creatures all around? He didn't want to be here.

In a quivering voice Sierra Ravenwolf cried, "Oh, this is too hard to leave this precious dog." Silent tears flowed down Carol's face too, and she turned away.

There was nothing else to do. Legally, Word was now a ward of the Pigs Peace Sanctuary. There he was to remain, without public contact, for the rest of his life.

Judy, sensing everyone's sadness, said, "Don't worry. I'll take good care of Word. He'll be OK in a little while when he gets used to the place."

At that moment, MooShu, a very clean, black, potbellied pig, came trotting up to Word. MooShu had lived at the sanctuary for four years and by general consent of all the animals was the chief greeter of the place. When any person or animal came to the sanctuary, MooShu would hear the gate open wherever he was and come running on his short, fat legs. Now he looked Word over. Then, sniffing from left to right, in a special language that animals have for each other, he grunted, "You are safe here." With that he waddled away.

While MooShu was greeting Word, Carol and Sierra Ravenwolf quietly left in the van. By the time Word turned to find them, the van had disappeared in the fog. Word, his tail hanging limply, felt terribly alone as he walked slowly down the driveway and fell in a black heap right next to the locked gate. His head turned toward the road, hoping the van would come back for him. He did not care that the ground was cold and damp, and he curled up a little more. The locked gate was an immediate comfort to him. After all, being locked up was what he had known for most of his life.

CHAPTER 8

A Different World

W ord was allowed to stay by the gate for as long as he wanted. Judy knew from past experience with animals and children that they all needed time to get used to a new place. After about an hour, Word began to move his head around, and his black eyes noticed things he had never seen before. This place was nothing like the shelter.

It didn't take long for him to become curious about his strange new home. He slowly picked himself up and began sniffing and looking around. The grass along the fence by the gate looked inviting and he walked over to investigate. He trotted along the fence, looking this way and that. Then he started to run. And run he did! He fairly flew along the fence. When he got tired he would rest, get up, and run some more.

That first night at the sanctuary, Word stayed out all night, even though it was a little chilly. He absolutely would not come inside the house, so Judy placed his food and water outside the back door on the porch. If being free meant staying outside as long as you wanted, then that's what he wanted.

During the next few days, Word came to learn about some of the other animals at the sanctuary. MooShu, the pig who had first greeted him, came over, and through an animal language that humans do not understand, gave Word information about the animals at the sanctuary. He let Word know immediately not to expect friendship with any of the animals at the sanctuary. Gossip had already spread around the place about why Word was there. By now all the animals knew he was considered dangerous and had harmed someone. Many of the animals were there because they had been hurt badly by someone and wanted nothing to do with a dog that was dangerous.

There was one exception, a little dog named Peter. Peter was a spunky little rust-colored Pomeranian who had been dropped off at the sanctuary after the old lady who owned him died. Peter had perky ears and a waving tail and was perfect in every way except he had only one eye. He had been born that way, but that didn't stop him from getting around the sanctuary.

At first, Word and Peter sniffed each other all over from end to end. Peter gave a friendly "Yip," and that's all it took. From then on, Word and Peter became best friends. All day they had as much fun as any two dogs could possibly have. Their favorite game was to run back and forth in the grass along the pasture fence, their ears flat and their tails bouncing over their backs. Word could run faster than Peter, so he would run ahead a little bit, turn around and bark to tease Peter. The two friends barked at each other in sheer delight. Another thing they would do was run around the farmhouse in opposite directions about three times and bark as they passed each other. They ate together, played together, and even slept together at the foot of Judy's bed. Wherever you saw Word, you saw Peter. They were inseparable.

It was MooShu who kept Word informed about the other animals. With a sniff and a snort, MooShu pointed to the animals and then gave a brief description of their personalities and how they had come to be at the sanctuary. Word, of course, had never been around pigs before and thought they were a lot like dogs. Some of the pigs could care less for any human attention while some of the others loved to follow Judy and the volunteers around just to be close and get a belly scratch.

Word learned that Gingersnap, a four-year-old potbellied pig, had been stuffed in a gunnysack and forgotten in the back of a pickup truck for two days without food or water. The terrified Gingersnap had finally been released in a field to be used as a decoy for hunters. After a difficult rescue to the sanctuary, Gingersnap became friends with Amos who had been found wrapped in wire and infested with lice. Word saw that both pigs ate and slept together and now had a good life.

MooShu told Word about another pig, Charlie, who had been found dodging cars on a busy street and running around terrified. He was now happy and safe. Holly, an older pig who was totally deaf, had been dumped in the woods. She had been rescued by Judy and was now content with her new pig friends.

Word learned that some of the animals had been so badly harmed that when they came to the sanctuary they stayed separate from the others for a while. Then they gradually begin to join in mealtimes and soon found friends. MooShu pointed out to Word that sometimes the pigs would "go camping" in the summertime when it got hot. Two or three of the pig friends, like Spud, Shelby, and Emily, would find a nice cool spot under a pine tree and sleep outside for the night.

Word followed MooShu to the barn where the smaller potbellied pigs slept on pig bedding of clean straw. There was a special door opening that led out to the pasture so the pigs could come and go anytime of the day and night. Next to them was another sleeping barn for the larger pigs that also had a special door opening to the pasture.

Word looked around curiously at all the new sights and pigs. None of the pigs paid any attention to him. Most of them edged away as he came near. He was totally ignored. They clearly wanted nothing to do with him. Word did not understand why all the animals avoided him, but at least he had Peter. At the thought of Peter, a happy feeling came over Word. One of the best things he did at the sanctuary was play with Peter. He loved to run with his friend along the fence and bark. They would run past the barn then down to the gate and do it all over again. He decided to find Peter, and this time they would start from the gate.

Unfortunately, the gate would prove to be a bad start for Word.

Chapter 9

Heart Break

Running back toward the gate with Peter, Word saw something that almost stopped his heart. He thought he saw Whip. No, that couldn't be. It couldn't be Whip. But it was Whip! It was his Whip, and he was calling his name! Word tore down to the gate, barking excitedly with tail flying, leaving Peter far behind. How could this be? Could this really be Whip after all these long years? To Word it didn't matter how many years had gone by, he could never forget Whip. He could never forget the man who had loved and cared for him and Mama. Now he was here! He was really here!

"Word! Here, Word! Come on, old boy," Whip called out in a husky voice. With that Whip leaned over the gate just in time to catch the joyous Word who leaped into his arms with a happy yelp. As he limped back to the car, Whip buried his wrinkled face into Word's silky black fur and whispered, "Oh, Word, it's so good to hold you again. I told you I'd come to take you home. And here I am."

Word gave Whip's face some sloppy kisses as Whip laughingly turned his head from side to side. For the squirming Word there was no happier feeling. How could this be? He was back in Whip's strong loving arms.

"Hey, Whip, hurry up! Let's get out of here before someone sees us," called Jim, Whip's longtime friend. "You got the dog, now let's go! We'll be in big trouble if anyone sees us. It's against the law what we're doing, you know that. We could end up in jail. This is really stealing, you know."

"I know, I know," said Whip climbing into the car. "Word is my dog and he'll always be mine. And I'm not stealing. He's my family. And I don't care what the courts say."

As the car backed up, Word turned his head to see a very sad Peter staring after him. The look on his face said, "Don't leave me, Word. Come back. Take me too!"

A funny feeling came over Word when he saw the sad-looking Peter. It was as if his heart split in two. One half of his heart wanted to be running with his friend Peter at the sanctuary, and the other half of his heart wanted to be right where he was—in Whip's arms. How was it possible to feel so sad and happy at the same time? There was a little blip in his heart as he decided to settle for the happiness of being with Whip for now. Thinking about the other part of his heart would have to wait for later.

Word's heart would have taken another blip if he could have heard the frantic phone call Judy made to Sierra Ravenwolf a few hours later after returning from a visit to the veterinarian.

"Sierra, this is Judy from the Pigs Peace Sanctuary. Something terrible has happened; Word has disappeared. He's gone," cried a worried Judy. "I'm worried sick."

"What happened to him?" asked a concerned Sierra. He couldn't have just disappeared."

"Oh, I don't know, Sierra," moaned Judy, "Word couldn't have gotten out of the gate. It's always locked. It was still closed when I came back from the veterinarian's office. Besides, he was playing with Peter. He would never leave Peter or this place. Word loves Peter, and he loves me. No way would he leave by himself."

"Then what do you think happened?" asked Sierra.

"I'm not sure," answered Judy. "I could get into big trouble over this. Remember, I signed a contract that Word is not supposed to have contact with the public. He's still legally considered dangerous, you know. If Word is found and someone takes him to an animal shelter, they'll discover the microchip in his ear. They will know that Word is dangerous, and he'll be destroyed immediately. Oh, Sierra, This is really scaring me. I'm worried, I don't know what to do."

There was silence at the other end of the phone for a minute. Finally, Sierra said, "Hmm, this is serious Judy. Let me think about it. I've got an idea. I'll get back to you."

Chapter 10

Sierra Returns

A knock on the door and a whiff of Lavender caused Word to start barking and dancing around like a top. There was no mistaking that fragrance.

"Be quiet," hissed Whip as he slowly went to the front door. "Calm down or I'll have to shut you in the bedroom."

There was no calming down Word. He knew who was at the door, and he couldn't wait for it to open. When the door opened, the beautiful Sierra Ravenwolf, standing there in a raincoat, said in a firm voice, "OK, Whip, I think you know why I'm here. I'm here for…what in the world have you done to Word?" she demanded. For staring up at her was Word, happy and dancing, but with a white stripe down his black coat. The white stripe reached from his head down to his back. It certainly did make Word look different.

"Uh, that's not Word," Whip said sheepishly. "It's my new dog, Pal. I know he looks a lot like Word, but he's different. They're the same breed is all. See this dog has a white stripe down his back. It's not Word."

"Yes, it is Word," said Sierra very firmly. "You're not fooling anyone. It may not look like him now, but what in heaven's name have you done to him, Whip?" asked a puzzled Sierra. "White stripe or not, it's Word alright." She reached down to pick up a very happy Word. "I'd know this precious dog anywhere and he knows me." At that minute Word reached up and licked Sierra's cheek. "Whip, I'm here to take Word back to the sanctuary where he belongs," Sierra announced.

It took a little more talking, but Sierra Ravenwolf finally convinced Whip. She pointed out that by keeping Word he was endangering Word's life and causing trouble for himself and others.

Whip finally admitted why Word didn't look the same. As he explained, he gently took Word from Sierra Raven-wolf's arms and placed him on his lap. "I got the idea from TV where some folks painted a stripe on their horse so no one could tell whose it was." He continued sadly, "I used a little white paint to make Word look different is all. It will come off easy."

During all the talking, Word relaxed on Whip's lap, happy that he had two of his favorite people close to him. "You know," Whip continued in a soft voice, "I've missed him terribly all this time. He is my family, and I told him that I'd come and get him and take him home. I don't care what those darn courts say. But now I can see I shouldn't have taken him. He's got a good life out there, I guess. I saw for myself that he was happy and well-cared for. You're right.

He should go back." A silent tear fell from Whip's cheek and landed on the white stripe of paint on Word.

"Here," he said abruptly, giving Word back to Sierra Ravenwolf. "Take him, and don't ever let anything happen to him either."

Back in Sierra Ravenwolf's arms, Word felt a splitting of his heart again. One part wanted to stay with Whip. The other part wanted to be back with Sierra and Carol at the shelter, and another part wanted to be at the sanctuary with Peter and Judy. Why was it so hard? Why couldn't he live with all the people he loved at the same time? It hurt to be taken from one place to another. It hurt in his whole heart.

It was a good thing Word could not know about more hurts coming to his heart.

CHAPTER 11

A Friend in Trouble

Word laid his head and front paws on Sierra's lap during the drive back to the sanctuary. He listened to her and tried to understand what had just happened to him again. She talked to him about Whip, the shelter, and the sanctuary. When she talked about Whip, she started laughing. "Oh, Word, you are a funny sight. I don't know what Whip was thinking. Imagine painting a white stripe on you!"

She laughed harder. "We were lucky he didn't paint you red or green." Again she laughed while one hand caressed his head. For the moment Word closed his eyes in total happiness.

"Seriously, Word," she said, "Whip painted you because he loves you and was trying to keep you safe. He's a good man. He fought for our country to keep all of us safe. I hope he finds another dog he can love. I think I'll call him tomorrow and tell him about the homeless dogs we have at the shelter. I'm thinking of one dog in particular that would be just right for him. Yes, that's what I'll do. I'll call him tomorrow. Anyway, Word, I have to tell you the truth. Whip can never see you again. It's just too painful for both of you. I'm sorry, but it's true. You are so much better off at the sanctuary, and I think you know that, Word."

As soon as Sierra drove up to the gate at the sanctuary, Peter started barking and jumping around wildly. Somehow he knew Word was coming back, and he was waiting to greet him. MooShu came waddling around to see what was happening too.

The paint came off Word easily, just as Whip had said. After that, Word settled into a happy routine. He played outside with Peter all day. At night they slept together at the foot of Judy's bed. As usual, he stayed inside when visitors came. Outside all the animals, especially the pigs, stayed far away from him. His happiest times were spent running with Peter in all kinds of weather at all times of the day.

One afternoon after Word and Peter had been running around, they headed for the water bowls inside the barn. As they were drinking, each in a separate bowl, Moses, the large Mastiff dog, also came into the barn for water. Moses was a huge, gentle dog weighing about 280 pounds. He had been with Judy for fifteen years and was dearly loved by everyone at the sanctuary. Because of his poor health, Moses couldn't hear or see too well. That day, for sure, he did not see Peter drinking out of his water bowl. As he lowered his massive head for a drink there was a loud "thunk," and a soft whine as Peter fell motionless to the barn floor.

Word stopped drinking, looked up first at Moses, then down at the lifeless Peter. What had happened to his friend? Quickly he moved to Peter and a slow chill came over him as he caught the smell of blood. Instinctively he headed for help and straight for the farmhouse and Judy, barking as loudly as he could all the way.

Judy was standing at the kitchen sink looking out the window. The minute she saw Word, she knew something was wrong. Constantly alert to all things at the sanctuary, Judy flew out the door and almost stepped on Word on her way out. She ran to the barn and saw Peter on the floor with blood all over. "Oh, what happened?" she cried out. Quickly she bent over Peter and touched the blood oozing from the side of his head. "Oh, no!" She repeated. She looked at Moses who was still slurping water, totally unaware of the accident. Seeing a trace of blood on his gray muzzle, Judy guessed what had happened. Carefully she picked up Peter, wrapped him in a blanket and headed for the van. Word ran right after Judy, barking frantically for his friend Peter. He wanted to be with him. Carefully, Judy laid Peter on the seat and said hurriedly, "No, Word, you can't come. I've got to get Peter to the vet as soon as possible. You stay here."

A worried and confused Word lay down by the locked gate and waited for Judy and his friend to come back.

It seemed like a very long time to Word, but after a few hours, Judy returned with Peter, who had a bandage over his eyes. The vet had explained to Judy that the bump on Peter's head had caused a serious injury to his eye. Peter was now totally blind. He said that Peter was fine otherwise and should be up and running in a few days.

In a few days, as soon as Peter could walk, Word became Peter's seeing-eye dog, guiding him all around the yard and barn. By gently leaning his body against Peter, he taught him to turn where needed. With nudges and soft yips, he was able to steer Peter safely all around the sanctuary. For one solid week Word worried about Peter and looked after his friend's every need. He did not leave Peter's side even for a minute.

The other animals at the sanctuary, aware of Peter's blindness, cleared a path whenever they saw the two dogs coming. It was quite a sight to see a dog guiding a blind dog.

At the end of the week Peter was able to get around the sanctuary all on his own. He bumped into the barn door a few times, but not enough to hurt. He always found the food and water bowls. Amazingly, by sounds and smells, Peter was able to find his way all around the place even though he was totally blind.

There was one big difference. Whenever Peter heard Judy's voice, he headed for her as if on a yo-yo string. From then on, Peter became Judy's shadow. Each time she went into the house, Peter followed or waited outside the door. He no longer wanted to go racing around with Word as they once did. He had a different way to live now.

Peter's recovery left Word with a feeling of emptiness. His friend didn't need him anymore, and he felt very lonely. He wondered what he should do. What was next in his life?

What was next was something he would not have wanted.

CHAPTER 12

Disaster

Something was wrong. Word awakened early with an uneasy feeling as he squirmed around at the foot of Judy's bed. It was just starting to get daylight, and for some reason he felt very uncomfortable. Judy was asleep, and so was Peter who was curled up in a ball beside him. Word lifted his head and shifted his front paws toward the cool fall breeze coming through the window. All his life Word could feel things he couldn't see. He could smell when things around him were changed or different. Even when he was a puppy, Word knew when Whip and his mama weren't feeling well. On this particular morning, he felt something was not right.

Suddenly, he knew what it was! It was a faint smell of smoke drifting through the window, and it was coming from the barn! With a bound and sharp, loud bark, he ran to the window and tried to jump up on the widow sill. Then back to the bed. He leaped on the bed and barked as loud as he could right in Judy's face.

"Word, stop it," Judy said crossly. "What are you doing?" Word jumped off the bed back to the window barking the whole time, and then turned back to Judy.

"Word," she called out, "What is it?" Sitting up in bed, she too caught a whiff of he smoke and screamed, "Oh no, the barn—it's on fire! The animals!" Quickly, Judy rolled out of bed, grabbed a robe, and raced down the stairs while slipping on shoes and dialing 911 on her cell phone. Word was a step ahead of her and out the door as it opened. He raced for the barn, barking as loudly as he could all the way.

Word did not need to be told what to do. He knew what to do. Through the barn door, with thick black smoke rolling out, he headed straight for the sleeping pigs. His barking, as he leaped around in the straw, caused an instant uproar of the frightened animals. All at once they tried to get out the door and away from him. Fortunately, both sleeping barns had special doors leading into a larger part of the barn that led out to the pasture. There was frantic squealing and rushing around as the potbellied pigs tried to find the way out of the barn. Because of the pigs' sizes, the rising smoke hadn't bothered them too much. It was the dangerous, barking Word they were trying to get away from. The pigs were smart, and their instinct was to go where they could smell the fresh air. Squealing and running, the pigs shoved into each other trying to make a distance between themselves, the barn, and Word.

Within minutes the fire truck arrived and immediately the sounds of gushing fire hoses mingled with shouts from the firemen as they began to control the fire.

Judy was outside in the pasture, still yelling out the pigs' names and counting them as they came out of the barn. She calmed down a little when she realized the cats were all out of the loft and the bigger pigs were out too.

Still inside the barn, above all the noise, Word heard a frantic yell from Judy outside. "There's one more! Dolly is in there! She's deaf and can't hear. I've got to get her." Judy, still in her robe, headed for the barn door, coughing from the smoke and yelling for Dolly. She was turned back by the stinging smoke pouring out the door. A fireman yelled at her, "Get back lady! You can't go in there."

"But there's one more pig inside! I've got to save her!" cried Judy.

"No!" commanded the fireman. "Get away from that door now!"

Word, still barking and jumping around in the mounds of bed straw, was gulping mouthfuls of smoke. The smoke that had risen to the ceiling was now settling on the straw, stinging his eyes. But he heard Judy yell there was one more pig in the barn. In the far corner he had seen a big lump of straw. It was Dolly! With her snout buried in the bed straw she had not smelled the smoke or heard a thing. She was sound asleep.

Word leaped over the mounds of wet pig bedding to the sleeping Dolly. He barked as loud as he could, but Dolly, being deaf, did not stir. Frantically, Word dug the straw away from her hindquarters and gave her a sharp nip. That did it! With a loud squeal, Dolly reared up, kicking straw in Word's face as she darted out of the smoky barn door.

From far away Word thought he heard Judy cry out, "Oh, thank goodness, Dolly, you're safe." With Dolly safely out of the barn, Word knew he'd better get out too.

By now Word wasn't sure where the door was. He couldn't smell fresh air anymore, and his eyes burned from the smoke. Barking hurt because of the smoke in his lungs. With all his strength he tried leaping over the wet straw. It was too hard. Maybe he would lie down for a little while and rest. With one last burst of energy he jumped in the direction he thought the door should be. With that leap his strength gave out, and panting heavily, he lay down on all fours to rest. From far away Word thought he heard Judy calling his name. He even thought he could hear Peter, who had been left behind in the farmhouse, barking for him. But the sounds were so far away. He was too tired and wet. It was too smoky, and he couldn't make his legs move anymore. Maybe he would sleep for just a little while.

It wasn't too long after that when a pair of very strong arms reached down and lifted his little black, smoky body out of the wet straw. "Well, what do we have here?" asked a fireman in a very tender voice. "It looks like we have a very brave, wet dog." Finding Judy, he gently placed the exhausted Word in her arms.

"Oh, Word!" Judy cried, as she kissed his nose and hugged him. "You are my hero, you precious dog. You saved the barn and all the pigs, and you saved Dolly."

Later Judy explained to the firemen that it was Word who had alerted her to the fire in the first place. And because of him, she had called for help and most of the barn and all the animals had been saved.

"You were very lucky the wind blew the smoke in the direction of the house and the dog smelled it," said the fireman. "If the wind had shifted the other way he might not have detected the smoke so soon. You would have lost everything. As it is, there's not much damage to the barn, only smoke damage. Another lucky thing is this little dog of yours chased the pigs to safety. Sometimes in a fire animals are too frightened to leave a barn because it's the only safe place they know. So they stay and lose their lives. Your dog saved the pigs by chasing them out. As I see it, your dog is a real honest-to-goodness hero."

Word did not hear the praise from the fireman. He was sound asleep in Judy's arms.

CHAPTER 13

The Unexpected

Within a week, the smell of smoke was replaced by the smell of new lumber and paint. Volunteers descended upon the sanctuary and were busy replacing the damaged corner of the barn. Their happy voices mixed with the sound of hammers and saws as the barn was rebuilt and painted in record time. Clean, fresh bedding straw replaced the soggy stuff in the pigs' sleeping barns, which made the pigs very happy.

The firemen explained to Judy that it was the old stove in the storeroom of the corner of the barn that had caused the fire. The stove was so old that the bottom had fallen out and ignited the wooden floor. It was a stove that had been in the barn long before Judy and the animals had come to live there. Some of the volunteers had started a fire in the stove while cleaning and did not know it was unsafe.

Word listened to the activity at the barn from his favorite spot on the front porch. Because of the legal contract Judy had signed, he could not have contact with the public, and that included the happy workers at the barn. It was a good thing he was not allowed out of the farmhouse gate. All the barking and running around during the fire had worn him out. He didn't feel like doing anything except sleeping anyway. He felt sad and lonesome. He was dog-tired.

The next day, after everyone had gone, Word wandered toward the barn. He was lonesome for Peter. But Peter wasn't around to play with anymore, and he would just have to get used to it. Since his blindness, Peter now followed Judy around most of the day, and Word was feeling like he had lost his best friend. It seemed all the people and friends he loved somehow always left him. There was Judy, of course, whom he dearly loved, and now MooShu had become a kind of a friend, and that was it. With tail and ears droop-ing, Word headed back to his favorite spot on the porch for another nap.

The nap made him feel better. He yawned, stretched his stiff front legs, then his hind legs. He was thirsty and decided to explore around by himself. He was free to do that now because everyone was gone and Judy was in the kitchen with Peter. Slowly he wandered across the yard toward the barn. He stopped. The burned corner of the barn and storeroom were now rebuilt and painted. It smelled and looked better than before, and Word knew it was a good thing for the sanctuary, especially for Judy who devoted her life toward the love and care of all the animals.

Moving closer to the barn, Word stopped again. He pricked up his ears and sniffed the air. Something very strange was going on. Something unusual was happening with the animals. He watched fascinated and without fear as all the animals in the yard began moving in silent motion toward him. The pigs sleeping in the barn woke up and came out into the yard toward him. The pigs eating in the pasture stopped and came forward. The llamas, Gus and Packer, and the horses came to the edge of the fence. The cats came out and sat on the edge of the loft without a sound. A funny feeling came over Word as he watched this most unusual behavior of all the animals. All the animals were moving toward him for some reason. Even Tom Turkey stopped strutting around and turned toward him. MooShu took a few steps forward and stopped with Dolly beside him.

THEN EVERY SINGLE ANIMAL IN THE SANCTUARY LOOKED STRAIGHT AT WORD AND SILENTLY GAVE HIM AN ANIMAL SALUTE!

For one magic moment there was not a single sound or movement from any creature as they gave Word their complete attention. Word instantly felt an invisible line from his heart to all of theirs. Their hearts talked back to him as they looked at him with a whole new look and feeling of acceptance. From their hearts to his, they let Word know he had earned their respect and was now one of them. It was a moment frozen in time and space, understood by every single animal in the sanctuary. Then, in the blink of an eye, the magic moment was over, and all the animals returned as they were before.

Totally stunned, Word just stood there. For a long moment he couldn't move as he tried to understand what had just happened. Whatever it was, it was wonderful and exciting. It was like being brand new all over again, inside and out. His heart danced inside with the new kind of love he had just received.

There was even a happy smell in the air, and the autumn sky became bright and sparkly. Word knew for absolute sure he now belonged to the whole sanctuary family, finally accepted by one and all. The eight long years behind the chain in the shelter were forgotten. His heart leaped for joy. With his tail and fur streaming, Word began to run for all he was worth. He ran and barked with such great happiness and delight that his paws barely touched the ground. He almost flew through the air.

Word was free! Word was loved! Word was home!

The End

To order additional copies of

WORD

Have your credit card ready and call:

1-877-421-READ (7323)

or please visit our web site at
www.pleasantword.com

Also available at:
www.amazon.com
and
www.barnesandnoble.com

Printed in the United States
205250BV00001B/289-294/A